MANATEE RESCUE

MANATEE RESCUE

NICOLA DAVIES

with illustrations by
ANNABEL WRIGHT

CANDLEWICK PRESS

Text copyright © 2013 by Nicola Davies
Illustrations copyright © 2013 by Annabel Wright
Illustration on pages 50–51 © 2013 by Robin Crossley

First U.S. edition 2015

Library of Congress Catalog Card Number 2014953073
ISBN 978-0-7636-7830-2

15 16 17 18 19 20 BVG 10 9 8 7 6 5 4 3 2 1

Printed in Berryville, VA, U.S.A.

This book was typeset in ITC Usherwood.
The illustrations were done in watercolor.

Candlewick Press
99 Dover Street
Somerville, Massachusetts 02144

visit us at www.candlewick.com

For Sarita and Tim

With thanks to support from a
Society of Authors' Foundation Grant

Chapter One

Manuela's paddle slipped in and out of the dark water without a splash. She steered the big dugout canoe between the flooded trees as lightly as a windblown leaf, never breaking the silent rhythm of her paddling. A flurry of small bats flitted over the water and disappeared into a tree hole, like smoke sucked back down a chimney. High above in the branches, a party of parrots quarreled. Manuela took no notice. All her attention was on the huge *renaco** up ahead, and the oil-dark water around it. The fig tree's green fruits were floating on the surface and being nibbled at from underneath by the pale shapes of fishes.

In the bow of the canoe, her father, Silvio, held up his left hand: the signal for her to slow down. Manuela didn't need to be told; she was already bringing the canoe to a stop within perfect range. Insects, frogs, and birds called all around, but the deep shadow of the fig tree held a perfect stillness.

Silvio shifted his grip on the end of the harpoon, and fixed his gaze on the flicker of fins and tails under the surface. Manuela held her breath. Silvio was a good fisherman, but when the river was this high, fish were hard to find. They had been out since before dawn and had caught nothing but a few little *bocachicos.**

The whiplash action of Silvio's sinewy arm was too fast to follow, but the bobbing of the harpoon in the water showed that he had struck a fish, and a big

---

renaco: a giant forest fig tree
bocachicos: mackerel-size fish, prized for their flavor

one. With three deft strokes of her paddle, Manuela brought the canoe alongside, and a moment later, a fat silver fish, bigger than a dinner plate, flapped in the bottom of the canoe.

Silvio hit the fish once with the handle of his machete, and it lay still.

"*Gamitana!*"* He grinned. "Not the biggest I've caught, but big enough. We can cook it with peppers and *celathro*.* You'll like that, won't you, Frog?"

The thought made Manuela's stomach growl. She looked at her father, and they both laughed. "Can we cook some *bocachicos* before we go home?" she asked.

"Of course! I think Frog and her papa have earned some breakfast!"

Silvio took up his paddle, and together they pushed the canoe out from the shade of the trees into the morning sunlight.

They put aside their paddles in the middle of a flooded clearing. All around, floating plants covered

---

***gamitana:** a large fleshy fish that feeds on seeds in the flooded forest
***celathro:** the local variety of cilantro

the water in a carpet so dense it looked like land. Manuela loved these clearings, shut away from all the world by their wall of trees. The only sounds were the booming call of a *camungo** echoing in the still air and the faint sizzle of the fish, over the little charcoal fire in a tin can. Manuela closed her eyes and let the sunlight warm her face. Fishing with her father was so much better than going to school. She was glad the council in the town, Puerto Dorado, had run out of money for diesel. Maybe the boat to school would never run down the river again!

Manuela's daydream was interrupted by a sharp hiss. Her eyes snapped open to find that her father had poured water over the fish and doused the fire. He was pointing at a small area of clear water, perhaps ten canoe lengths away. At its edge, a patch of floating plants quivered, and the faintest of ripples spread over its smooth surface. Underneath the water, something big was moving.

Silvio turned to her over his shoulder and silently mouthed a word: "Manatee!"

**camungo:* a large black-and-white bird with a loud, mournful call

Manatee! Manuela's heart raced, her hunger forgotten. She had only glimpsed a live manatee once before, and never this close, close enough to hunt.

"Not everyone can kill a manatee, little Frog," Silvio had always told her. "Only the most skillful."

There was a law against killing manatees, but out here, so far from town, no one took any notice of it. Catching a manatee was too special to bother with what the police two hours downriver might have to say about it. When someone brought in a manatee, the whole village got excited. There was so much meat that whoever caught the creature could trade it for almost anything.

But Silvio hadn't caught a manatee for a long, long time. They were getting scarce. Sometimes, in the dry season, when the rivers and lakes shrank, somebody speared one. Sometimes one would drown by accident in a net, or a calf would be caught alive and sold in the town downriver.

Manuela had always dreamed that one day she and her father would bring home a manatee. Then people would say how *skillful* she was and not how strange it was that a *girl* should go fishing with her father. She would be a heroine instead of a freak. Here at last was her chance!

"Manatees are very wary," Silvio had always told her. "They can hear a bare foot shift in the bottom of a canoe."

So Manuela slid her paddle slowly, slowly between the floating plants and pushed smoothly against the water's resistance. Her senses were on high alert. Colors were brighter and even the tiniest sounds rang out: the scratch of a dragonfly's feet as the insect perched on the gunwale, the *plink plink* of grasshoppers, jumping to avoid the canoe's stealthy progress.

Up ahead, the manatee's nose broke the surface. It was so easy to miss: just a disk of flesh with two black nostrils set in it, no bigger than a coin. It took a breath, making a soft *pfff*, and was gone.

"Remember," her father had told her, "they swim backward after taking a breath, so if you throw a harpoon in front, you'll likely miss it."

Manuela pointed the canoe behind the spot where the nose had appeared. They were almost close enough now. One more careful paddle stroke turned the craft to the side, to give them clear shots. Silently, Manuela put down her paddle and took up her own harpoon.

The pool was a smooth, dark mirror again. Silvio and Manuela waited, their harpoons poised and ready to throw. A jacana* screeched as it flew low over the floating mat of plants, its legs trailing, and the *camungo's* mournful booming began again. Still they waited, eyes straining, muscles tense.

There! A minute swirl on the surface, not quite a ripple, not quite a bubble. No ordinary person would even see it, but Silvio knew it was the trail of a tail, moving underwater.

Manuela caught the flick of Silvio's arm from the corner of her eye. Her own arm, already on a hair trigger, shot like a coiled spring. Silvio's harpoon struck. It had been thrown with such force that

*jacana: a waterbird with huge feet and claws

when it hit the animal, it shivered with the shock of the impact. Just to the side, Manuela's struck, but glanced off and lay floating on the surface. Then Silvio's harpoon, upright and stuck in the manatee's body, disappeared as the creature dived.

"It will come up again in a moment," Manuela's father said. "Then we'll have it!"

They both took up their paddles and were at the the spot where the manatee had dived in a moment. Blood blossomed in the water, but there was something else, too.

"Father!" Manuela cried. "There's a little *cria*.* Look!"

A bristly nose showed above the surface, and a small dark body bobbed beside the canoe. But the calf was wounded. There was a bloody cut slanting across its shiny black back.

"You must have scraped it as I hit its mama," said Silvio. "Quick, put a rope around its tail. Then we can be sure the mother will come back!"

---

*cria: the Spanish word for the young of an animal

Chapter Two

Manuela had imagined that killing a manatee would be like killing a very big fish, just more exciting. But it wasn't at all. The manatee mother fought hard and took a long time to die. Her calf tried to get up close to her, even after she was dead, when Manuela and her father were straining to roll the vast body into the canoe. The sun was already sinking by the time they managed it.

"If we put the *cria* next to its mama, it might wriggle out of the boat," Silvio said, looking at the huge corpse. "You'll have to hold it on the way back while I paddle alone."

Manuela nodded but said nothing. The long, gruesome struggle had changed how she felt about manatees. Killing them wasn't heroic or exciting. It was just horrible.

The calf lay very still in the water, but it squirmed a little when Silvio lifted it into the boat.

"It's pretty small," he said. "I don't think it's more than a couple of months old."

The calf didn't *seem* small to Manuela when Silvio put it in her arms. It was as heavy as her cousin Valerio — and he was a solid little boy of nearly two.

She held the baby with its round tummy against her chest, its paddle tail curled onto her lap. Its funny, bristly nose rested on her shoulder. It didn't wriggle at all, but its nostrils opened and closed as it breathed, and its eyes, like little chips of polished charcoal, blinked. The skin of its back was tough and rubbery, but underneath its flippers, it was like velvet, the softest thing Manuela had ever felt. It was odd that an animal without arms or legs could feel so much like a human baby.

"Do you think he will live?" she asked her father.

"Don't know, Frog." He sighed. "That cut on its back is bad. I *hope* it lives, because Jose Gomez will buy it for a good price and sell it to some government official as a pet."

Jose Gomez brought basic supplies from Puerto Dorado in his big, fast boat and sold them in Manuela's village, San Larenzo, for a high price. Everyone knew that he would do anything for money. They called him Clink-Clink because of the way money was always jangling in his fat pockets.

Gomez fished too, with his three sons, but unlike Silvio, they used nets.

"It takes no skill to use a net!" Silvio would grumble.

"It may not take *skill,* brother," Silvio's older brother, Luis, would answer him, "but it catches fish."

Luis was right. Gomez's nets caught enough fish to sell in Puerto Dorado. And, seeing how well the nets worked, other fishermen, like Uncle Luis, had begun to use them, too. But nets didn't just catch

11

fish. They caught other things as well, by mistake: river dolphins, turtles, and manatees. A baby manatee had been caught in Gomez's net last year and he'd sold it for a lot of money. Afterward, Manuela had heard that it died.

Manuela hoped the cut would discourage Jose Gomez from making a deal. She didn't want this calf to die, too.

Silvio paddled the canoe through the flooded forest and then out onto the milky-brown river. Manuela watched the rhythm of his paddle strokes and remembered the story her grandfather Mauricio had told her about manatees.

"There are certain ceiba* trees — big, big trees where fat caterpillars feed," he'd said. "And when the caterpillars drop into the river, they turn into manatees!"

Manuela loved this story. Even though Mauricio had drowned when she was small, she could still recall his voice. She'd dreamed of watching caterpillars drop into the water and becoming manatees.

---

*ceiba: a giant jungle tree, rare now due to logging

But this little calf had not dropped off a ceiba tree. It had come into the world the same way she had, from a mother's belly.

All the long way home, Manuela stared down at the dead mama manatee and felt sadder and sadder. The curve of the animal's tail was just under Manuela's feet, and her bloodied head touched the seat where Silvio sat to paddle. The pale patch on her chest stood out in the evening light like a bright island in a dark lake. Her flippers were folded on her chest, the way old ladies folded their hands in their laps.

In her head, Manuela told the mama manatee how sorry she was that they had killed her. *I'll make your baby well,* she told the mama. *And I'll put him back in the river one day. I promise.*

She whispered to the calf, "Don't die! Please don't die!" And in her heart she named him Airuwe. The word meant "manatee" in Ticuna,* her grandfather Mauricio's language.

---

*Ticuna: a native people of the Amazon and the language they speak

Chapter Three

It was dusk when they got to San Larenzo. Yellow dots of lamplight showed at the doors of the houses, reflecting on the floodwater that had crept up between them. The forest behind the houses was one vast shadow, and the floating raft, where boats tied up, was almost invisible against the dark water. Everything seemed asleep, but the village faced the river and there was always a pair of eyes somewhere watching. When Silvio yelled out for help as they got close, Uncle Luis and his two sons, Jorge and Gonzaga, came out in their boat with the motor and towed them in.

Luis slapped Silvio on the back, and there was a lot of laughing.

"Who needs nets to make money, eh?" Silvio teased.

Luis's nickname in the village was Take-It-Easy, so he ignored his brother's teasing. "You just got lucky, Silvio," he said. "It doesn't mean I'm going to stop using nets to fish any time soon."

Jorge's fine loud voice called out across the water, "Manatee! Manatee!"

By the time they got to shore, half the village had gathered to take a look.

Silvio was exhausted from paddling the heavily loaded canoe, but he stood up in the stern and raised his paddle in triumph over his head. This was the moment Manuela had dreamed of — returning home with a manatee that she had helped to hunt and kill. But something inside her had changed. It was as if a switch had been flicked on. So when Silvio turned to her and said, "Only the most skillful catch the manatee, Frog, and that's us!" she couldn't return his smile, and only whispered to the calf not to die.

There were plenty of hands to help get the dead manatee out of the boat. Everyone was excited about eating something that wasn't fish for the first time in weeks. From the moment it was hauled out, people began bargaining.

"How about a new propeller for that broken-down outboard of yours, Silvio?"

"I have two bags of farina* to trade. . . ."

"How much meat for half a drum of gas, Silvio?"

For the time being, Manuela and the baby were forgotten.

A dog pushed its way through the crowd and looked down at Manuela from the edge of the jetty. It woofed a greeting and danced into the canoe, its tiny claws chittering on the wood. It sniffed at the manatee's tail and growled.

"No, Tintico!"* Manuela scolded. "Be nice! Where's your mistress?"

There was a thud of feet, then Libia, Manuela's cousin and her best friend, landed in the canoe.

"Right here!" Libia announced.

Libia was tiny, like her miniature pet. She was stunted and wizened, with one leg shorter than the other because of a disease she'd had as a baby. On land she walked awkwardly, but in a canoe she was as quick as a fish. Her mind darted like a fish,

*farina: In the Amazon, *farina* refers to a coarse meal made from cooked and ground-up cassava, a starchy root. It is added to almost everything and also eaten alone.

*tintico: Colombian Spanish slang for a small cup of dark coffee too—she was full of crazy ideas. Other kids were wary of her, which made her Manuela's natural ally. She was another girl who didn't behave the way little girls were supposed to.

Libia crouched beside Manuela and put her skinny hand lightly on the calf's side. "How can something that feels like a rubber mat be so cute?" she exclaimed.

Manuela smiled. It was true. The manatee was a bit like a big rubbery slug, yet there was something irresistibly lovable about it.

"I've named him Airuwe," Manuela said, "and I'm going to take care of him and put him back in the river when he's grown."

Libia raised her eyebrows.

"I thought you wanted to hunt manatees, not be their mama!"

"I did," Manuela said sadly, "but not anymore."

"What does your dad think?" Libia asked.

"Papa wants to sell him to Gomez."

"I see," said Libia. "Then we may just have to do some manatee kidnapping!"

Silvio was calling loudly for Manuela, so there was no more time to talk.

"Where is my daughter, the great hunter?" he cried.

Many hands picked Manuela and the calf out of the canoe and put them on the jetty. People patted Manuela on the back and cooed over the calf.

"This is our big day, Frog!" Silvio beamed. "We caught a manatee and its calf."

Silvio was so pleased and proud. Manuela didn't want to oppose him, but right then her promise to Airuwe seemed more important than pleasing her father.

Clink-Clink came puffing down the jetty toward them, and Manuela's heart fell as her father tried to take the calf from her arms. She held on tight.

"Papa, don't sell the manatee to Mr. Gomez, please."

Silvio's smile disappeared. He looked astonished, as if wondering why his daughter was behaving like this. She was always so practical. They always agreed on everything.

"But, Frog, he'll give us a good price," Silvio said, bewildered. "Come on, give it to me!"

Manuela shook her head.

"Do what your father tells you!" Gomez barked. "Hand it over!"

"But look, he's wounded!" Manuela showed

Mr. Gomez the cut on the calf's back, but he just shrugged.

"It's only got to survive as long as it takes to get it to Puerto Dorado tomorrow. Once I've sold it, it can die as much as it likes." Gomez laughed.

Manuela saw how much Silvio disliked what Gomez said. *There's still a chance,* she thought.

"Please, Papa, please let me keep him. I'll take care of him, I promise."

But Silvio wouldn't meet her eyes. "No, you can't keep it!" he said coldly. "Gomez is giving us good money for it."

Manuela had never heard such a chill in her father's voice. She felt as if she had been slapped, but the hurt made her even more determined.

"This is not an *it*!" she shouted. "It's a *baby,* and you shouldn't buy and sell babies!"

"You see," Gomez told Silvio, "this is what comes of teaching a girl to fish and hunt!"

Into this angry space, Libia suddenly appeared with Tintico in her arms.

"Come on, Frog," she said gently. "Just give the *cria* to Mr. Gomez, eh?"

Manuela glared at her, harsh words about betrayal springing to her lips, but there was a glint in Libia's eyes that said, *I've got a plan.*

"Well," Manuela said, "only if you take really good care of it."

Silvio snatched off his cap in relief. "Good girl!" he said. "Thanks, Libia."

Reluctantly Manuela put Airuwe into Mr. Gomez's arms. The calf wriggled and made a plaintive little sound that pinched her heart. She hoped Libia's plan was a good one.

Mr. Gomez wore a nasty, triumphant smile on his face as he carried the manatee away. Silvio glanced guiltily toward Manuela, but she was already halfway up the path toward Libia's house, with Tintico dancing in front of them in the lamplight.

Chapter Four

Libia's house was always full of people. That was why Manuela liked it so much; her own home had just herself and her father in it. Manuela's mother, Fernanda, had died soon after she was born, and Silvio had never found another woman he loved as much as the beautiful girl he'd brought home from his wanderings in Brazil. He had concluded that he would never have another child, which was why he took Manuela out in his boat.

"If I can't teach a *son* to fish, then I'll teach a *daughter*," he always said.

It made people tut and roll their eyes, but everyone knew that Silvio Castello was a bit *loco*.

There was always someone fighting, cooking, sleeping, sewing, singing, or dancing — and very often all of those things together — at Libia's house. Tonight, several big brothers were sitting outside fixing nets and exchanging jokes with Libia's dad, Abel. There were medium-size sisters doing each other's hair, while a gaggle of small children were playing a complicated game of chase. Libia's mother, Angelina, was crooning a song to her newest baby and dancing around the room with him in her arms. Like her big brother Silvio, Angelina was considered a little eccentric by the village, but Manuela liked the way she sailed through the chaos of her home and the way she let Libia run as wild as she pleased.

"*Hola,* Manuela!" Angelina called dreamily as the two girls came through the door.

"*Hola,* Auntie Angelina!" Manuela called back.

No one else took the slightest notice of them, so Libia, Manuela, and Tintico went through the house and out the other side to the quiet corner of the veranda where Libia slept.

Libia lit a candle in a jar and sat cross-legged on the floor, with Tintico on her feet. She pointed to a thin pole, stuck in the water at the bottom of the veranda steps. Along its length were stripes of different colored material. There was something a bit offbeat about it that was typical of Libia.

23

"That," Libia said proudly, "is a color-coded flood map of San Larenzo!" She grinned. "It tells me exactly which parts of the village are flooded and which parts I can get to in a canoe, depending on which color stripe the water reaches. After the rain last night, it got to the red stripe."

Libia paused as if Manuela were supposed to know what that meant.

"Which *means*," Libia went on, "the water reaches all the way to Gomez's place, so we can paddle a canoe from this veranda to the back of his house!"

Manuela suddenly felt a lot more awake. "So when everyone's asleep, we take your canoe and steal the manatee back!"

"Exactly!"

All over the village, the smell of cooking manatee began to rise into the evening air. Manuela hoped the little calf couldn't smell it, too, or if he could, wouldn't understand what it meant.

* * *

Manuela often stayed over at Libia's, so no one asked any questions about the two girls whispering together out on the veranda. When at last the net fixing, hair braiding, chasing, dancing, singing, and baby cooing had died down and the house fell silent, it was easy for Manuela and Libia to sneak down the veranda steps to Libia's canoe, which floated on the floodwaters at the back of the house. Tintico came, too, tiptoeing down the wooden steps as if he understood the need for secrecy.

The thick, rainy-season clouds had been gathering all day and now blocked out the stars. Manuela and Libia were used to paddling around the village in daylight, but finding their way in utter darkness was not so easy. Manuela was glad the constant plinking and churring of frogs and insects covered the sounds of the canoe bumping into submerged trees and other people's boats. A trip that would have taken twenty minutes in daylight took them more than an hour. At last, a little break in the clouds gave them some light. The blazing tropical stars showed a plastic tank, the bottom half of a rainwater barrel, on the last patch of dry ground behind Gomez's house.

The canoe scraped against the shore. Manuela got out and scuttled to the tank. She could hear the little manatee buffeting itself against the walls of its plastic prison. At least he was still alive.

She reached into the tank, but it wasn't so easy to get hold of him. Airuwe wriggled and splashed, the noise reaching the ears of Gomez's dogs. They began to bark, more and more loudly. Any second now, lights would flash on — Gomez had a generator and electric light for his house — and that would be that.

With one last desperate effort, Manuela plunged her arms into the tank and managed to grab the manatee. She pulled him out and made for the canoe, half running, half stumbling. The baby was heavier than she remembered, and she was glad to lay him down on the two pillows they had put in the bottom of the dugout and cover him with a wet sheet to keep him comfortable.

"Let's go!" she hissed to Libia, and they pushed the canoe out into deeper water.

Behind them, the dogs barked madly and Gomez shouted at them to shut up.

For a few minutes the girls just paddled, relieved and delighted to have gotten away with the manatee. Then Manuela suddenly realized that this was as far as Libia's plan had gone. Neither of them had thought of where they might take a kidnapped manatee calf in the dead of night.

"We could run away to Peru," said Libia.

Manuela sighed. Sometimes Libia was just crazy. But there was one place they *could* go. "We'll go to Granny Raffy's," she said. "Who else is going to help us?"

Although Granny Raffy's house, which everyone knew as Riverbend, was not really part of San Larenzo, it was downstream and easy to find. Even without paddling, the girls knew that they would probably get there, as the river always seemed to wash things up at the little inlet where Granny had made her home. All the same, it was scary. Neither of them had ever been out on the river without an adult, even in daylight. They clung to the bank, afraid of the power of the river farther out and watching fearfully for the glint of caiman* eyes in the starlight. Then the clouds closed over and the fierce stars were gone. Rain pelted down, leaving them groping along in the dark, poked by overhanging branches, and afraid.

*caiman: a kind of crocodile

Just when Manuela was sure they must have gone too far and were lost, the sound of music played on an old windup gramophone came to them through the falling rain. It sounded like an orchestra playing under the river. They *were* in the right place — and Granny Raffy was still up!

Chapter Five

Granny Raffy was Silvio's mother. She had come to the Amazon to work in the hospital in Puerto Dorado for six months and fallen in love with Silvio's father, Mauricio. He was a Ticuna, one of the tribe who had lived beside the Amazon forever, and she was a city girl.

"It'll never work," people said. But Raffy and Mauricio got married, and Raffy never went home. She was the only trained nurse that San Larenzo had ever had, but she'd made Mauricio build them this house away from the village so that only people who were really sick would make the effort to come to see her.

"I've had enough of every kid running to me with a bruised knee," she'd said.

When Mauricio drowned, Silvio had tried to get her to move back into the village, but she wouldn't. She loved the river and the jungle, she told him. She wasn't so sure about people.

Raffy was bossy and tough, but with her on your side, you could win almost any battle. Although she was old, she was still spry and feisty, and when she saw the little dugout draw up to her half-flooded jetty, she rushed down to meet her granddaughters, scolding them all the way up the steps to her house. *What were they doing out on the river at night? Didn't they know how dangerous it was? What would Silvio and Angelina have to say? Did they know just how much trouble they would be in? Whatever were they doing with a half-dead manatee calf?*

Since she'd moved out of San Larenzo, Raffy had started to heal animals as well as people. Right now, there was a baby sloth with a bandage around one leg hanging over her veranda and a couple of macaw chicks in a hat on a table. Silvio said she was nicer to her animal patients than she was to her human ones. So the girls weren't surprised when she cradled the manatee in her arms, calling him a "poor little mite," while growling at them and bossing them out of their wet clothes. She fired questions like bullets until they had told her the whole story of the capture and "kidnapping" of the calf.

Then Raffy ordered Libia and Tintico straight to bed, as their skinny little bodies were shivering and they were both clearly exhausted. "At least you're a bit bigger and stronger," she told Manuela, "even if you are *stupid* enough to go out on the river in the dark. Now let's see what we can do for this calf."

Raffy led Manuela into the room she used as a clinic and laid the manatee on the table there, cushioned by an old blanket.

"You'll have to hold him while I clean the cut," she said.

Manuela did her best, holding the manatee's tail under one hand and its body under the other. She noticed the gentleness with which Raffy's expert nurse's fingers worked along the calf's wound with a pad soaked in disinfectant. The calf wriggled and made a little peeping sound.

"Keep him *still*," Raffy barked.

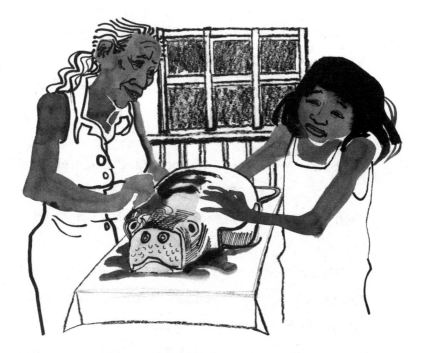

In the light, Manuela could see how bad the cut was. Even though it had happened hours ago, it still oozed blood.

The calf squeaked again, and Manuela winced in sympathy.

"Huh! It's all very well feeling sorry for it now, Frog," Raffy exclaimed. "I bet you and Silvio were glad enough to harpoon it."

Manuela said nothing. Raffy was right—she *had* wanted to hunt manatees all her life, but *catching* one had changed all that in a day. The calf's little sounds of pain felt like words of reproach. "Will he live, Granny Raffy?" she asked at last.

Raffy looked up at her granddaughter, suddenly less gruff. "Perhaps, *china*,"* she said. "But then what, eh? I don't think you know what you've started."

Raffy gave the cut one last wipe. "There, that's the best I can do," she said. "Let's put him somewhere he'll be more comfortable."

Together they dragged the *lavadero*—a plastic tank like a bath that Raffy washed clothes in—onto the far end of the veranda. They filled it from one of the water tanks that caught the rain from the roof. Raffy added hot water from the stove because, she said, rainwater was a lot colder than the river and the river was what the calf was used to.

Held down on the table, the calf had seemed very like a rather tired caterpillar, but when Manuela

china: Colombian Spanish for girl

slipped him into the water, he became a manatee again. His nostrils closed and he submerged, then popped his nose back up with a little puff of breath. "Hmm!" Raffy smiled. "Maybe his chances are better than I thought."

Raffy told Manuela that manatees, like many baby animals, could not drink cow's milk. They needed special milk powder that you could only get in Puerto Dorado. She had a little that she'd used for other young orphaned animals that should work. She put some in a baby's bottle and gave it to Manuela. "Try to make it eat," she ordered. "I'm going up the hill to see if I can get a signal on the phone, so I can let Luis know you aren't drowned."

Manuela nodded. Uncle Luis had a cell phone, and everyone in San Larenzo used him as the village messenger. He often fished at night and got a clear signal out on the water.

When Raffy had gone, Manuela sat alone in the dark, leaning against the side of the bath. She was very tired, but she knew she shouldn't fall asleep. Even if the baby recovered from the wound on his back, without food, he would die very soon.

The night sounds of frogs and insects and the high hunting calls of bats were all around. Far off, the sky flashed pale with distant lightning, and rain pattered on the tin roof.

Airuwe was investigating his new home. It was a cramped space, even for so small a calf. He could turn around, but only by scraping his tail on one side and his nose on the other. He did this twice and then came to a halt with his head near Manuela's end. She could hear his bristly nose whispering against the plastic. She slipped her hand into the water and began to touch the manatee's side with her fingers. At first he flinched a little, but he didn't move away. Slowly, she began to rub Airuwe's skin. She worked her hand along the folds of his chin and under his jaw. Gently, so gently, she eased his head upward and with her other hand lifted the bottle and pushed the teat toward his mouth. His upper lip — strong and mobile, like a hairy finger — felt the teat, investigating this new object. Manuela held her breath, hoping Airuwe would taste the milk and start to suck. But instead he spat out the unfamiliar teat and turned his head away.

Over and over again, Manuela tried to persuade Airuwe to try the milk. But each time he pulled away, Manuela learned a little more about the geography of his face and mouth and how he moved. At last she was able to push the teat firmly into his mouth and hold his chin with the other hand. He tried to twist away, but Manuela kept the teat in place just long enough for him to taste the milk. To her delight, he began to suck.

"It's OK," she told him. "Things won't always be as bad as today. You won't always live in a washbowl. Just get well, and one day I'll put you back in the river."

By the time the bottle was empty, Manuela could feel sleep overtaking her. She lay down by the tank, too tired to find anywhere more comfortable. As her eyes closed, she wondered what Granny Raffy had meant when she'd said, "I don't think you know what you've started."

Chapter Six

At first light the next morning, Manuela began to find out.

She opened her eyes and saw Silvio at the other end of the house, pacing up and down like a jaguar stung by wasps, arguing with Raffy. Manuela decided to shut her eyes and stay still for a little longer. Silvio didn't get angry very often, but when he did, it was scary.

"The manatee *has* to go back to Gomez," Silvio growled, banging his fist on the veranda rail and making it jump.

Raffy didn't flinch. She went on feeding the baby macaws with banana mush from a spoon. "Why?" she said calmly. "Since when did anyone in my family do what that creep Jose Gomez tells them?"

"Mama, you're *impossible.*" Silvio's voice was white-hot with anger.

Raffy calmly answered right back, "No, Silvio,

you're impossible!" she said. "Just *look* at that child. That's where she fell asleep last night. *That's* how much she cares about this creature. And you are going to reward her bravery and determination with betrayal? As if it's not enough she's growing up without a mother."

"Should I reward her for stealing?" Silvio was

actually shouting now. "And is it my fault my wife died?"

"Well, it certainly *is* your fault you didn't marry again," Raffy replied calmly.

There was a crash, and Manuela half opened one eye. Silvio had kicked Raffy's chair.

"That's it. That's *it*," he cried. "I'm leaving."

"Good!" said his mother sharply. "But you aren't taking your daughter or the manatee with you."

"I don't *want* my daughter," Silvio snapped. "I just came for the manatee."

Manuela heard Silvio's feet running down the steps with a sound like a whole row of faces being slapped. She kept her eyes shut until the growl of the outboard had faded.

"You can stop pretending to be asleep now," Raffy said, "and feed your manatee. They're like human babies and need to be fed every few hours. You'll need to change its water and clean the cut with disinfectant, too. Libia can help you. Come on, get to it."

Raffy stalked off to the kitchen, shaking her head. "That Silvio!" she said with a sigh. "Just as much of a hothead as he was at sixteen."

The manatee wouldn't come near the bottle when Libia offered it, but she didn't mind. "You're the manatee mama," she told Manuela, "not me." So she and Tintico sat back and watched.

Manuela held the calf's chin in one hand and the bottle in the other, and on the fifth attempt, the teat went in and the calf began to suck. The level in the bottle fell, then stopped falling, and the calf's charcoal-and-ash eyes closed.

"He's fallen asleep!" Libia said. "My baby brother does that. Mama has to wake him up to keep him feeding."

"How does she do it?" asked Manuela.

Libia giggled. "She tickles his feet."

Airuwe didn't have feet, only flippers. These felt too hard to tickle. Then Manuela remembered the softness of his "armpit." Everyone was ticklish there. Manuela put her hand into the water and tickled under the calf's right flipper. It worked at once, and the calf woke. She pushed the teat back into his mouth, and the milk soon disappeared.

Then the water needed changing and Airuwe's cut had to be cleaned. It took them a while to figure out how to do this. First they scooped out most of the water with a bucket, then Manuela held him still while Libia cleaned his cut. Then Manuela lifted Airuwe out of the tank so Libia could pour out the last of the water, her skinny limbs shaking with the effort.

"Yuck," Libia said. "That water stinks. How much pooping can one baby manatee do?"

"Lots." Manuela laughed. "We'll have to change his water twice a day at least, Raffy told me."

"Why so often?" asked Libia.

"We have to keep the cut clean," Manuela replied. "Anyway, you wouldn't go swimming in your own poop, would you, Libia?"

"Well, *we* swim in the river and *that's* full of

poop from every village upstream," said Libia.

Sometimes Libia said things that drove Manuela crazy, because they were right and wrong at the same time. Manuela was about to say that the biggest river in the world was quite a lot larger than a bath, but Airuwe was squirming too much. She put him back in the tank, and together the girls refilled it, bucketful by bucketful, carefully mixing in warmer water from Raffy's stove.

It had taken more than two hours to feed the calf, clean his wound, and empty and refill the tank, so when Raffy called them to come and eat breakfast, they were ravenous.

Raffy's fish stews were delicious. The girls piled on the farina to soak up the juices and dug in.

When they'd finished eating, Raffy sat opposite them and looked hard into their faces, her eyes glinting like sun on the water. "So, girls," she said, "what is your plan for this manatee calf?"

Libia just opened and closed her mouth like a landed fish, but Manuela answered quietly, "I promised his mama I'd make him well and put him back in the river."

"And what do you think Jose Gomez is going to say to that, my girl?" Raffy replied. "Or your father, for that matter?"

Manuela looked at her feet. It *did* sound silly when she said it aloud. But in her heart it felt right.

"And where is your manatee going to live before it goes back to the river?" added Raffy. "He can't stay in my *lavadero*."

"Maybe he could live in your old fish pond, Granny?" Manuela suggested.

"Hmm." Raffy grunted. "You'll have to clean it out first. But that's not the only problem. He'll need to be fed on milk for month, and that costs money. A *lot* of money. And it takes time. So you need a plan."

Manuela studied the dirt between her toes.

"Even if you keep your promise," Raffy went on, "and put him back in the river, what then? A fisherman could kill him a minute later."

Manuela didn't have any answers. This was what Granny Raffy always did: asked questions that made you realize you didn't know what you were doing. That was why she always made Silvio and even Take-It-Easy Luis so angry.

The buzz of an outboard down on the water signaled that Raffy was about to get her first patients of the day. "I'll be busy all this morning by the looks of things," she said, "but you need to come up with a plan, fast. And if you can't, I'll take that manatee to Gomez myself."

Chapter Seven

M anuela and Libia sat together on the veranda, watching the manatee's nose poke through the water's surface and disappear again. Manuela sighed. Even if Papa and Mr. Gomez backed down, and they could clean out Raffy's pond for him to live in, where would she and Libia find money for the special milk powder? And would they be able to keep feeding him for months? Even if there were solutions to those problems, to truly keep Airuwe safe forever, she would have to ask all the fishermen in the village not to hunt him. And he could never really be safe if his friends and relatives were hunted, so they would have to stop hunting *all* manatees.

"Maybe my promise is too big to keep," she whispered.

Libia looked glum and didn't answer.

The girls sat in gloomy silence.

Tintico grew bored. He trotted around and around the bath, sniffing. Finally, he got up on his hind legs, his face reaching just over the edge to where Airuwe's nose popped up. The two noses sniffed each other intensely. Then, the manatee poked his head right out of the water and his tiny, twinkling eyes took a good look at the little dog. Tintico wagged his tail and "uffed" a greeting, and the manatee submerged with a splash, so suddenly that Tintico got water in his nose and spent the next minute sneezing. The girls laughed.

"We can't give up," said Libia, "not now that Tintico likes the *cria,* too!"

Manuela smiled. Libia was right. They couldn't give up yet. Even if her promise was much bigger than she had at first understood and much, much, *much* harder to keep.

It took the rest of the morning and some of the afternoon — through a rainstorm, two more bottles of milk for Airuwe, and another emptying of his home — but at last Manuela and Libia had a plan.

"We should write it down," said Libia. "Granny will be more impressed if we do that."

Manuela made a face. Paper and pens were not a big part of their world, but she knew Libia was right. Granny Raffy had been educated in the city, and she was *always* writing things down.

"I'll borrow Raffy's pencil and one of her notebooks," Manuela answered. She did so, and they set to work. The result was a bit untidy, but it did have pictures of people and manatees and drawings of leaves around the outside:

Manatee Action Plan

1. **Clean out Granny's fish pond for calf to live in.**

(That was the simplest part of the plan. Granny used to keep fish in her pond to eat, but now it just grew weeds.)

2. **Make money to buy special milk: carry things in Libia's canoe; sweep paths in the village; collect empty bottles for Mr. Gomez.**

(This was more difficult. No one in San Larenzo really had much money, but Granny Raffy always seemed to have enough, although her patients hardly ever paid her. Secretly, the girls hoped that she would get the milk for them.)

3. **Make people like manatees more, but not to eat. Ways to do this: invite people to see calf; tell people there are not many manatees left.**

4. Get people to agree not to hunt manatees.

(This was the most difficult part of all. People had always hunted manatees. Until yesterday, Manuela herself had wanted to hunt them. She wished she could put into words how she had felt watching Airuwe's mother fighting for her life. That would be enough to make anyone stop hunting manatees.)

5. Return manatee to the river. Find out where manatees like to live and the best place to put him.

(They thought hard about this one. They knew manatees lived in the river, but not everywhere in the river, especially now that there were so few. Libia covered the big gap in their knowledge with an especially large picture of a manatee mama and her calf.)

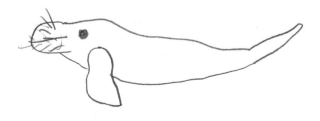

* * *

In the middle of the hot afternoon, Raffy rested in her rocking chair on the veranda and the girls stood anxiously before her. Manuela knew that if she didn't like their plans, then she really *would* take the baby to Gomez.

Raffy examined their paper, smiles and frowns chasing their way across her face like clouds in a windy sky. "OK," she said at last, "this *is* a plan. So I won't take the manatee to Gomez."

The girls grinned at each other with relief.

"But," Raffy went on sternly, "it's very, very short on detail and I don't know how you're going to make numbers three and four happen. But I can help with number two if you do some chores around here. I have to buy more milk powder for other animals anyway."

Libia and Manuela exchanged tiny smiles while Raffy was looking down again.

"There is something you haven't thought of that might help with numbers three and four," Raffy went on. "You should name the manatee. People will care more if he has a name and he'll be easier to talk about."

"Manuela's already done that," said Libia, hopping around with excitement. "Remember what Grandpa used to call manatees, in Ticuna?"

"Airuwe!" Raffy exclaimed. "You named him Airuwe?"

As Manuela nodded, she saw tears in Raffy's eyes — even though Raffy said it was just dust.

Chapter Eight

Raffy crossed out *Manatee* and wrote *Airuwe* at the top of the action plan and pinned it to the wall by the front door. The next morning, the girls made a start on number one.

Clearing out the old fish pond for Airuwe to live in was harder than they expected. Raffy hadn't used the pool since Mauricio had died, and it was choked with weeds and full of green water. It took the girls all day to pull out the weeds and scrub the pond clean, in between feeding Airuwe and cleaning his tank.

Refilling the pond was a problem, too. Raffy had an old hand pump, so they could pump water from the river, but it was really slow and hard to use. The pond was still only half full by the end of the afternoon. Then Raffy suggested that they set up two huge tarpaulins to run rainwater into it and help to fill it up.

Overnight, rain hammered on the veranda

roof and cascaded out of the gutters. By morning, Airuwe's new home was full enough to put him in, as soon as the sun had warmed the water a little.

The sun was out as they carried Airuwe down to the pool. He had been much more wriggly when they'd taken him from the bath, and Manuela didn't want to risk him falling from her arms, so they carried him in a wet sheet, holding it like a sling between them. Tintico gamboled alongside, sniffing at Airuwe through the fabric and "uffing" encouragingly. When they got to the pool, they lowered the sling in and waited for the manatee to swim out into his new home. But he didn't move.

"What's the matter with him?" said Libia. "Doesn't he like the pool?"

Manuela looked down at the calf and saw, instead, herself as a baby: alone in her crib and longing for the comfort of her mother. Without another word or thought, she slipped into the pool and eased Airuwe out of the sheet and into the water. She floated beside him and he cuddled in close.

"I know how it feels," she whispered to him. "I know."

"You really are a manatee mama," said Libia. "Here, give him his bottle."

The water came up to Manuela's shoulders. She put one arm around Airuwe and held the bottle to feed him with the other hand. His face was out of the water and close to hers. He looked at her carefully. This time, he didn't fall asleep once and finished a whole bottle in half an hour.

Airuwe got more used to being fed from a bottle. He would accept it from Libia and Raffy, but it was only Manuela he liked having in the water with him. He grew stronger as his wound started to heal, and he began to explore his pond. He made use of different parts of it at different times of day, depending on whether he wanted the warming power of the sun or the cool of shade.

Like the parents of small babies, Manuela and Libia fell into a routine of feeding times and sleep.

Granny Raffy helped out when she didn't have patients to see and sometimes did the nighttime feedings so the girls could get a proper sleep. In return, they helped with Raffy's chores, feeding the macaw chicks and the sloth, cooking, and cleaning. Neither Manuela nor Libia had ever spent so much time with Granny Raffy, away from the village. Libia missed her brothers and sisters and the bustle of her busy home, but Manuela felt she now understood why Raffy liked living at Riverbend, where every day began with a storm of little green parrots in the treetops and ended with Granny Raffy's gramophone music drifting over the dark river.

Angelina came to visit. She didn't tell Libia off at all for disappearing in the middle of the night. In fact, in her dreamy way, she seemed to have forgotten altogether about how the manatee had come to be at Granny Raffy's. She was quite happy for Libia to live at her granny's house for a while, at least until the boat to school started running again.

Uncle Luis visited, too, with Gonzaga and Jorge.

They brought a share of their fish catch and the supplies that Granny Raffy had ordered from Puerto Dorado, including big bags of milk powder for the hungry manatee.

Luis said that Gomez was trying to pretend he'd sold the calf in Puerto Dorado, but that everyone in San Larenzo knew what had really happened. People were thoroughly enjoying the fact that Clink-Clink had been outwitted by a couple of kids.

Manuela worried that Gomez would try to take the calf back.

"He'd have to get past Raffy first!" Luis laughed. "Anyway, he wants to save face. My guess is that he'll get his money back from Silvio and forget the whole thing."

"Is Papa still angry?" Manuela asked.

Luis nodded.

"Are you angry, Uncle Luis?"

"Me?" Luis grinned. "You know me, Frog. Me and my boys, we take life as it comes. Silvio's a hothead, but he'll cool down. You'll see."

But Silvio never showed his face nor sent any message, and Manuela wondered if her father would be angry with her forever. Had he really meant it when he'd said that he didn't want her?

Libia decided that Airuwe needed to go to school. "He needs to learn about all the other creatures he'll be sharing the river with, like fish and caiman and dolphins," she told Manuela one morning while her cousin was in the pool with the little manatee.

This was a typical piece of right-but-wrong Libia-ness. Manuela raised her eyebrows but said nothing.

The next morning when Manuela came to feed Airuwe, there was a long pole leaning over the pool with several models made of sticks and plastic packaging dangling from it.

"That's a *gamitana,* that's a *pacu,** and that's an electric eel," Libia said.

They looked a little *like fish,* Manuela thought, *if you looked with your eyes half closed and your head*

pacu: a species of large fish, similar to the *gamitana*

on one side, but not enough like the real thing to teach Airuwe anything.

All the same, Libia added to Airuwe's "school" every day: more fish, a turtle, and even a pink dolphin, although that was made from chicken wire and cardboard, so it could not be left out in the rain. Tintico growled at the models, and Airuwe took no notice of them at all.

"He doesn't even look at them!" Libia said, disappointed.

"Never mind, Libia," said Manuela. "I like them."

Libia smiled. "You know what, Frog?" she said. "You're much nicer now that you're a manatee mama."

Even though Airuwe didn't look at Libia's school, Raffy's patients did. The dangling models attracted their attention, and pretty soon the pool had become Raffy's waiting room. Airuwe and his school prompted people to talk about their lives beside the river: the biggest fish their father caught when they were little, or the time they found a huge nest of turtle eggs, or when a hoatzin* landed in the canoe.

*hoatzin: a big bird with a crest on its head

They told stories, too, about tapirs* turning into manatees and dolphins coming out of the river to take human wives. But most of all they talked about Airuwe, about what a fine creature he was and what a shame it was that there were so few manatees nowadays. Perhaps, one old fisherman suggested, it was because there was no longer the right sort of ceiba tree for manatee caterpillars to eat.

"I think we've made a start on number three on the action plan!" Manuela whispered to Libia.

"Yes." Libia smiled. "This is a school for humans, not manatees, after all."

The rainy season continued, and the river rose toward its highest level. One evening, Raffy sat with the girls beside the manatee pool. Towering clouds reflected the setting sun onto the surface of Airuwe's watery home. His wound had healed into a white flash over his back, like a streak of lightning, which showed clearly when he was close to the surface.

*tapirs: pig-like forest mammals with a long snout

"Will the scar fade?" Manuela asked her granny anxiously.

"I'm not an expert in manatee scars, *china*!" Raffy replied. "But I don't think so."

"It'll make him so easy to hunt!" Manuela almost wailed.

"But it'll make him really easy to tell from other manatees!" said Libia.

"Either way," Raffy said, "if you want to keep your promise, you'll have to work more on number four of the action plan. I think you should start by inviting everyone in San Larenzo to come and see Airuwe and his school. Who knows? Silvio might even come."

Chapter Nine

Manuela was amazed that Granny Raffy, who didn't really like lots of people all together, was prepared to have the whole of San Larenzo tramping over her property. But she kept her astonishment politely to herself. The next day, Raffy gave the girls paper and crayons, and they set about making posters to advertise "Meet-the-Manatee Day," which would happen on the following Sunday. They decided that Libia should catch a ride back to San Larenzo in Uncle Luis's boat, so she could pin up the posters all over the village and tell everyone about it.

Luis came by in the afternoon and dropped off Raffy's supplies. He was in a big hurry and ran up and down the steps with the bags and boxes.

"What's the rush?" Raffy asked.

"Don't you ever look at the sky, Mama?" Luis laughed and pointed at the black clouds. "I don't want to be bailing rainwater all the way home!"

He hustled Libia and the bag of posters into the boat.

After so long in Libia's company, Manuela felt lost at the thought of being without her cousin. They waved and smiled at each other as the boat pulled away. Tintico ran to the stern to keep Manuela in sight for as long as possible.

As Manuela and Raffy walked back up to the house, giant raindrops began to fall.

"I think Luis is still going to be bailing, for all his hurrying!" Raffy said.

Rain in the Amazon is not like rain anywhere else on earth. Raindrops are fatter and wetter, they fall faster, and they are more tightly packed into the space between clouds and earth. By the time Raffy and Manuela reached the house, they were drenched and gasping for breath. Water had taken over the space where air normally was. They stood on the veranda, their voices drowned out by the deluge hammering on the roof, smacking into the ground, and slapping onto the millions of leaves in the forest.

Raffy had to put her mouth right next to Manuela's ear in order to be heard. "Wait for the rain to ease off before you feed Airuwe."

Manuela nodded and sat down under the cover of the veranda to wait, while Raffy went for a siesta.

But the rain did not ease off. After an hour, Manuela decided that she couldn't make Airuwe wait any longer for his food. She made up a bottle and yelled to Raffy that she was going, forgetting that Raffy would not hear her above the noise of the rain.

The jungle, the river, *everything*, had disappeared in a sheet of gray, so it took Manuela a moment to see what had happened to the pool. The floodwaters, which had been thirteen feet or more away from Airuwe's pond, had risen so suddenly that they had engulfed it. The pond was no longer an island of water in dry land, but simply another part of the river, only visible as a square of deeper water at the edge of the flood. And there was no sign of Airuwe.

Manuela immediately plunged into the flooded pool to look for him.

The rainwater was cold, and Manuela gasped as it hit her skin. She dived again and again, searching the pool by touch. But there was no rubbery skin, no bristly nose. If Airuwe had swum out to join the river, he could be swept away. Without a mother to feed and protect him, he would die.

Manuela struggled back to the shore, picked up Airuwe's bottle, and waded back into the water, as deep as she could, while still keeping her feet on the bottom. Then she tapped the bottle with a stick—she did this every time she came to feed Airuwe, and he had learned to associate the sound with food. She tapped the bottle repeatedly, pushing back the tears that started to squeeze into her eyes.

The water was rising fast, and the current was beginning to pick up, tugging at her legs. The rain still lashed down, blurring the water and the forest into a smudge of gray. Seconds passed like hours, minutes like weeks, and still there was nothing.

Then — *pppff* — Airuwe's nose popped through the surface right in front of Manuela! His solid, round body hung in the water next to hers. He was too big now for her to hook an arm over his back, so she held tightly to a flipper with one hand and put the teat into his mouth with the other.

The current was threatening to push them over. Using the bottle to tempt him, Manuela shuffled backward into shallower water, where she could get some anchorage to prevent them both from being swept away. But she had forgotten that the pool was just behind her, and she went in over her head. When she kicked back up to the surface, she found that she was still holding the bottle and that Airuwe was still hanging on to his dinner! She swam on her back, kicking hard with her feet and trying to pull them both closer to shore, but the current swirled them farther out, closer to where the river rushed as fast as a galloping horse.

Something banged against Manuela's shoulder: a branch! She let go of the bottle and grasped the branch tightly, pulling herself and Airuwe toward it.

Other branches caught at her legs and slapped her face, but they held Manuela and the manatee like rice in a sieve as the floodwater sluiced past.

As long as Manuela could hold on to Airuwe with one arm and the drowned tree with the other, they would not be lost. But they were not out of danger. The new floodwater was so very cold, and baby manatees could die in cold water. Manuela shouted a few times but soon gave up. Calling for help was useless — Raffy would never hear her above the storm. She would just have to hope that her granny would notice that she had gone and come to look for her.

Manuela stretched her arm as far around Airuwe as it would go. At least he didn't wriggle. In fact, he seemed to want the comfort of her presence. She shut her eyes and felt the rain beat on her head.

"Frog! Frog!"

Silvio's voice was calling her!

Manuela opened her eyes and there he was,

leaning out of his boat and tying a rope around her. Raffy was at the stern, handling the outboard. Silvio's thin face was full of worry and streaming with water.

"What are you doing here?" Manuela gasped.

"Rescuing you, what do you think?" he said.

It was almost dark. Manuela realized that she must have been here for hours. Her arm was still around Airuwe.

"We'll tow you to shore," Silvio said. "Hold on to Airuwe."

Back in shallow water, Manuela's legs were almost too chilled and weak to hold her up, but she kept her arms around the manatee.

"We'll get him in the *lavadero*," said Silvio. "Then we can drag him away from the water until the flood's gone down."

"We must warm him up," added Raffy. "He's too cold."

"And so are you, Frog," said Silvio. "Let go of the manatee and go inside."

Manuela shook her head.

Silvio and Raffy exchanged a look.

"OK," Silvio said. "Let's get this done."

Manuela wouldn't leave Airuwe until he was safely in the tank. Then Raffy ordered Silvio to take her inside.

"Papa," Manuela whispered as he scooped her into his arms, "did you mean it when you said that you didn't want me?"

"No, Frog," Silvio said softly. "Of course I didn't."

Chapter Ten

Morning was like a different world. The rush of rainwater had subsided. The pool was once more surrounded by dry land. The sun shone. By the time Manuela woke up, Airuwe was back home in his pool and the *lavadero* hung on its hook at the far end of the veranda.

Some things hadn't survived the flood. All that was left of Libia's school were the soggy remains of the pink dolphin, wrapped around the tree trunk.

"Libia will be upset," Manuela told her father. "The models weren't very good, but they got people talking."

"I could make some models if you like," Silvio offered. "I was a good woodcarver when I was a kid. Luis, too."

Manuela looked at her father, her eyebrows knotted. "Aren't you angry with me anymore?"

Silvio smiled. "A bit. I didn't expect my little Frog to grow up so suddenly and fight me!"

"I'm sorry, Papa," Manuela said.

Silvio shook his head. "No, you did what you thought was right. And you made me think, not just about this little baby, but about *all* manatees. What if there were no more manatees? No more *pirarucus*?* No more *pacus*? Already there are few, but what if there were none, *no more*?" Silvio blew out a long breath and shook his head. "That would be a terrible, *terrible* thing."

"Does this mean that you won't let Gomez take Airuwe?" Manuela asked quietly.

"You know, Frog"—Silvio smiled—"I've never much liked Clink-Clink. Come on. I'm going to find some wood and carve a fish."

Everyone from San Larenzo came to Meet-the-Manatee Day. They came because they were curious about the Castellos—the family of eccentrics who had lived among them for two generations: Nurse Raffy and her animal patients; Silvio and his dead Brazilian beauty; Manuela and Libia, the two

---

*__pirarucus:__ large Amazonian fish, up to 6 feet (2 meters) long

ungirlish little girls who had pulled a fast one on old
Clink-Clink. Seeing the baby manatee was just an
excuse.

But when they arrived at Riverbend, manatees
were hard to avoid. There were homemade manatee
posters and pictures everywhere in the house and

on the veranda. There were even plates of manatee-shaped cookies with little signs saying: EAT ME, NOT A REAL MANATEE! Along the path leading from the back of Raffy's house, there hung wooden carvings of fish and turtles, giving a manatee's-eye view of the river. There was even a puppet show, put on by Angelina's middle-size daughters, with a pink dolphin in a hat, a sassy sloth, and a lost manatee *cria*.

The San Larenzons loved it. They couldn't remember when they'd had a better time. And to their surprise, the best thing of all was the manatee himself. Most people had eaten manatee, and many had killed them or seen their dead bodies lying in the bottom of canoes. But to see one alive and close up, to watch it swim and turn its white-patched chest to the sky, to look into its strange little eyes and see them looking back, was new. They sat beside the pool smiling, exclaiming, quietly entranced. They simply *loved* Airuwe!

Only one thing spoiled the day, and that was Jose Gomez and his two thuggish sons. They turned up toward the end of the afternoon and laughed nastily at everything. Some people, who owed Gomez money or who thought he was an important man to impress, laughed with him, but most people turned away. They were growing tired of Clink-Clink and his bullying swagger.

Manuela was in the water with Airuwe, while Libia, who loved to perform, sat beside the pool and answered the many questions people asked about Airuwe and his adventures. Tintico pranced around, part of the show.

When Gomez arrived, Libia's great-great-uncle Misael was talking to the girls. "I'll bring you some food for your *cria*," he told them. "It looks like he's big enough to begin to eat his greens and leave the milk behind, and I know the plants that Airuwe likes."

Gomez disrespectfully pushed straight past the old gentleman to speak to the girls. Airuwe slipped under the surface, the white flash of his scar showing clearly through the water.

"So you're making money from *my* manatee, eh?" said Gomez.

"We're not making any money, Mr. Gomez," said Manuela.

"Yeah, sure." He smirked. "Well, just remember that he's *mine*. And I *will* have my property, one way or another."

Silvio stepped up behind him. "He's not yours, Jose," he said mildly. "I gave back your money."

"You did me out of a profitable deal, Silvio," Gomez replied, "and I won't forget it." He threw a manatee cookie into the pool. "I'll be eating the real thing, thanks," he said, "and so will everyone else. Just you wait and see!" Then he stalked away with his sons, their noisy engine roaring behind them.

"Don't take any notice," Silvio said to the girls. "He's all talk."

But Manuela wished that Gomez hadn't seen the scar that marked Airuwe's back.

Chapter Eleven

After Meet-the-Manatee Day, Raffy put a big check mark beside number three on the action plan. They had definitely made people like manatees more, and not to eat. The space beside number four stayed blank, however. No one had *promised* not to hunt manatees, even if they liked them.

Libia's great-great-uncle brought a selection of floating plants for Airuwe, just as he had said he would. He called it *farinha di manati* and said it included water hyacinth, water lettuce, and tender new grasses. He told them that he had seen manatees eating all these plants and more. But, he added sadly, he hardly saw manatees at all now.

Manuela put the plants in Airuwe's pool and hoped that he'd know what to do. At first, Airuwe took as much notice of the plants as he had of Libia's models, but every time Manuela gave him a bottle, she brought the plants close to his mouth and "nibbled" at them with her fingers. In a week, he began to nibble, too; in a month, he was eating a few handfuls every day and drinking a little less milk. Manuela could see that the day would come when bucketloads of plants would replace bottle feeding. Then Airuwe would be ready for number five, whether there was a check mark next to four or not.

Uncle Misael got some of his old fisherman friends to help. Airuwe was so used to the bottle by now that Misael and his cronies could even feed him. They started spending some afternoons at Airuwe's pool, taking turns with a bottle or watching the manatee eat the food they had collected for him.

Libia's Manatee School got bigger and bigger as carvings of all kinds began to turn up at Riverbend. The people of San Larenzo were competing with one another to see who could make the most life-like models of fish, turtles, caimans, and even huge pink dolphins.

Silvio, Luis, and Abel built a thatched roof from which the models could hang. Now, when people came to see Airuwe, they could walk among the models just as manatees swam among real fish in the river. Raffy began to get used to the fact that visitors arriving by boat at her jetty were as likely to want to see a manatee as a nurse!

The school boat began to run again. Now that Airuwe's care was shared among several people in the village (Raffy, of course, drew up a schedule), Manuela and Libia had no excuse not to go back to school with everyone else. But students and teachers wanted to know all about Airuwe; for the first time the girls were popular with other children. A visit was arranged for the whole class. Children from other villages, where fishing was not as important as in San Larenzo, loved the Manatee School, and the teachers said that they would bring children to see it every year, even if Airuwe was back in the river.

Manuela still went out on the river with Silvio, but she never missed school to do it anymore. There was a reason to work at her studies now: she wanted to find out more about manatees and the other animals that lived in the river. She began to think about other action plans, for turtles maybe, or *pirarucus,* and asked Silvio for help. Her father nodded and said that many creatures had been hunted too much and that there were fewer now than when he had been a boy.

Libia decided that she was going to write puppet plays about animals for children, and she spent all her spare time sewing puppets with her sisters. She made a special Airuwe puppet for Manuela, with a line of white wool stitched down its back to resemble his scar.

As Airuwe grew bigger, so did his circle of friends. All Manuela's family visited to help clean out his pool or bring food. Fishermen came by with new carvings or just to see how Airuwe was doing. Raffy made her jetty bigger so more boats could tie up safely and even admitted that before Airuwe came, she'd sometimes been a bit lonely.

People told Manuela and Libia about creatures they had seen: dolphins, big fish, even birds, as well as manatees. Libia began to keep a record of what everyone saw out on the river, because she said that it might help them to find the best place when the time came for Airuwe to go back to the river. Now, on the school boat in the morning and the afternoon, all the children had their eyes peeled for animals and birds, and a small check mark appeared beside "Find out where manatees like to live" on the action plan.

There was still no check mark beside number four, but sometimes changes happen too slowly to be checked off anyone's list.

Chapter Twelve

Manuela visited Airuwe whenever she could. Sometimes, Libia and Tintico came, too. The manatee still seemed to know Manuela and would come to the side of the pool and push out his bristly snout when she dangled her feet over the edge.

One afternoon, Manuela was rubbing Airuwe's back with her hand when Raffy came down to the pool and sat beside her. "So," she said in her usual direct way, "isn't it time that you kept your promise and got to number five on the action plan?"

"But we haven't checked off number four yet!" Manuela protested.

"That's true," said Raffy. "But Airuwe has so many friends now that I think it's safe for him to go back."

Manuela knew that her granny was right. It wasn't fair to keep Airuwe in this little pool when he could be free to wander the river. She nodded.

"Yes, it's time."

The whole family wanted to help return Airuwe to the river.

Libia consulted the records in the journal and chose a place where manatees had been seen. Luis offered his big boat to take them there. Gonzaga, Jorge, Abel, and, of course, Silvio said that they would lift Airuwe into the boat, and Angelina said she had an airbed to protect him from bumps on the journey. They set the day and agreed to meet at Riverbend early in the morning before it grew too hot.

Manuela and Libia stayed with Raffy the night before, on the floor of Raffy's room. Manuela lay awake in the first light, staring at the fading stars through the window.

"You're awake, aren't you?" Libia whispered.

"Yes."

"Should we go and say good-bye before everyone gets here?"

The sky was pearl gray, and the sandbanks on

either side of the low river showed like pale arms in the early light. Birds called and the last bats flitted in the shadows.

They hadn't visited Airuwe at this time since he had been a little calf, needing to be fed milk every few hours. Now he was a big grown-up, much larger than the two girls put together. His smooth, dark shape lay under the water, partly covered by a wreath of his favorite foods.

The girls knelt at the edge of the pool, with Tintico between them, and Manuela tapped the water with her fingers.

Pppff.

The familiar bristly nose broke the surface, then Airuwe's whole head came to rest on the side of the pool between the girls, nose to nose with Tintico. His small eyes looked out at the world of dry land. For a moment everything held quite still, and then the sound of approaching motorboats broke the quietness.

It wasn't just one boat, or even two. Almost the

whole village of San Larenzo had turned out to help their friend the manatee. Only Gomez's boat was missing.

Manuela wished that Airuwe could understand what was happening to him. The trip in the boat would be frightening, and when they let him go, he might feel very alone. But she knew that he would soon feel at home in the river, where he should have been all this time.

They passed a tarpaulin under Airuwe's body to act like a sling, then drained the pond. He was bigger than anyone had imagined, so it was a good thing that all the strongest men in the village were there to help. They lifted him out of the pool as gently as they could, then over the sandbank and into the boat. Airuwe rested on the airbed and was wrapped in wet sheets to keep him cool and comfortable. Then they set off, a fiesta of boats full of smiling, singing people, with one bewildered manatee at its heart.

Manuela sat beside him all the way. "It's going to be all right," she told Airuwe. "You're going home."

Epilogue

For weeks after Airuwe was gone, Manuela said, "Stay safe, Airuwe. Stay safe!" every night when she lay down to sleep. But as weeks turned to months, more and more people told her or Libia or Silvio or Raffy that they had seen a manatee with a mark like lightning on its back. Little by little Manuela stopped worrying and began to feel that Airuwe was safely back in his true home.

More than a year later, Manuela was on a sandbank with Silvio and a group of kids from Silvio's new Ecology Club. They were searching for turtle nests to move to a safe hatching place where they couldn't be dug up for food by anyone passing by on the river.

It was fun running around on the sand looking for the telltale signs of turtle tracks. The smallest boy in the group, whom they all called Ant because of his size, was the best at it. He and Libia waved to

Manuela from the far end of the bank, calling out that they had found a nest.

But there was something distracting Manuela's attention: a boat, big and fast. It was Gomez's boat, not coming upriver as usual, but down from the lakes, where manatees spent the dry season. It wobbled in the heat haze, but Manuela could see Gomez's eldest son at the helm and Gomez in the bow. He was shouting at the top of his voice, "Manatee! Manatee!"

No one ran down to the boat. No one helped carry the huge body onto the bank, so Gomez and his sons butchered the animal on the river and brought the meat up in batches.

The three men stood next to the bloody pile on the stranded jetty as Manuela, Libia, and the other children walked past carrying the turtle eggs.

"Told you I'd get my property in the end," Gomez taunted. "That nice white scar was a great target."

Manuela stared at the bloody chunks of the manatee's body, searching for a telltale streak of white on black skin. But there was nothing, just meat and blood.

Silvio came up the bank like a rocket.

But Manuela caught his arm. "Don't hit him, Papa," she said quietly. "There's something much better you can do while we take care of the eggs."

Gomez shouted until he was hoarse, but no one wanted to buy the manatee meat. He and his sons had to carry it the length of the village and run their generator to cool it in a fridge.

Meanwhile, Silvio quietly went to every house and every boat, seeking everyone's opinion. When he knew that the whole village felt the same, he went to see Luis. "We need to make a call on your phone, brother," he said.

Luis nodded. "The number for the police is in the memory."

Killing manatees had been illegal for years, but it was impossible for the police to know what went on in all the little villages along the river, unless someone told them. Now someone had.

Gomez was given plenty of warning. Luis told him that it would take the police launch at least two hours to get to San Larenzo. That was easily enough time for Gomez to load his boat with manatee meat and his two sons and leave. Forever. Which is exactly what he did, watched in complete silence by every family in San Larenzo.

As Gomez disappeared up the shrunken river, shouting threats and insults until he was out of earshot, Silvio put his hand on Manuela's shoulder. "No one in this village will ever kill another manatee," he said. "Not ever."

But her heart still felt like a stone.

In the five years that followed, fishermen up and down the river often saw a manatee with a white scar on its back. And if they had been thinking of throwing a spear, they changed their minds. No one wanted to kill the famous Airuwe.

But Manuela told herself that Airuwe was dead.

Granny Raffy didn't believe it. "You didn't *see* a

white mark on that corpse," she'd say. "Gomez just *pretended* that he'd killed Airuwe to spite you."

Manuela shook her head, but she couldn't quite shake the hope out of it.

Then, one day, when Manuela, Libia, and Ant were coming back from a village downriver where they'd been performing one of Libia's puppet shows, their outboard failed. They paddled into a lagoon to fix the engine.

It was a beautiful sunny afternoon. Little grasshoppers plinked on the floating vegetation, a damselfly landed on the gunwale, and a *camungo* boomed sadly in the reeds.

"One nice thing about a broken engine," Ant joked. "We get some peace!"

On the opposite side of the lagoon, floating weeds trembled, and there was a minute swirl on the surface, not quite a ripple, not quite a bubble.

Manuela pointed.

"Manatee!" she said. *"Manatee!"*

Pppff!

A snout with two nostrils kissed the surface. Below, in the still, shadowy water, there was a flash of white, like the memory of a summer storm, passing in a long lost sky.

Manuela's heart sang.

I kept my promise after all, she thought. *I kept my promise to Airuwe.*

LIVING WITH MANATEES

There are three different kinds of manatees: West Indian, West African, and Amazonian. They and their close cousins the dugongs are the only water-living mammals that eat plants. They have two front flippers and a paddle-shaped tail.

Manatees are big, slow-moving animals, which means that they burn energy much more slowly than other mammals and so can't keep warm in cold water. They can only survive in water that stays above 68°F (20°C) all year round.

Their eyesight is poor, but they can hear well. Touch-sensitive bristles surround their mouth and help them to find the right plants to eat, and muscled lips gather the food into their mouth. Eating plants wears down their teeth, but manatees shed their worn teeth at the front; they're replaced with new ones from the back.

Manatees can live for thirty years or more. They have just one baby at a time, with a gap of three years in between. A baby manatee stays with its mother for up to two years and doesn't have babies of its own until it is between six and eight years old.

The manatees in this book are Amazonian manatees. Unlike dugongs, which live in the ocean and are happy in fresh or salt water, Amazonian manatees live only in fresh water, in the Amazon River and the rivers that run into it. Amazonians are the smallest manatee but can still be 10 feet (3 meters) long and weigh 1,100 pounds (500 kilos). Other manatees are gray all over, but the Amazonian manatee has darker, more rubbery skin and a big white patch on its chest.

The Amazonian feeds in a different way from its relatives, too. In the murky waters of the Amazon, there's too little light for plants to grow under the surface, where other manatees find their food. So Amazonian manatees feed mainly on floating plants, nibbling at them from underneath or sometimes poking their heads out of the water.

Water levels in the Amazon can vary between the wet and the dry season by as much as 46 feet (14 meters), which is nearly twice as high as an average two-story house. In the wet season, the river floods the forest and there's a lot of surface where floating plants can grow. Manatees eat a lot and get fat! But in the dry season, the river shrinks, and manatees must retreat to lakes or deep parts of the river, where the water stays deep enough to hide them. They survive there by living off their fat reserves.

Unfortunately for manatees, in addition to being big and slow-moving, they also taste good to humans, rather like pork. So everywhere they are found, manatees have been hunted. They also get tangled up in fishing nets, injured or killed in collisions with the propellers of motorboats, and poisoned when rivers are polluted. Their low breeding rate means that manatee numbers can't recover quickly if too many are killed.

Amazonian manatees have been hunted by humans for at least five hundred years, especially in the dry season, when many manatees can be found together taking refuge in lakes. They can be herded using boats and then speared or caught in nets. Sometimes, many manatees are killed at once.

Calves, orphaned when their mothers are killed or caught in nets because they were too young and inexperienced to avoid it, are sometimes kept in captivity until they are big enough to eat or are traded as pets.

There are more motorboats and nets in the Amazon than ever before, and manatees are now an endangered species because people still hunt them, even though it's illegal.

One way to keep manatee numbers from falling is to return orphaned calves to the wild, which is happening in many parts of the Amazon. But the hunting and careless use of nets still continue, and calves are still orphaned.

The real problem is that in places where food and money are scarce and the police can't see what's going on, it doesn't work to *tell* people not to kill manatees; they have to *want* not to.

In Puerto Nariño, a small town on the Amazon in

Colombia, an organization called Natütama has been working with local people to encourage them to love manatees and not to hunt them.

Natütama's work began with a real-life incident very like the story in this book. An injured manatee calf was rescued and passed on to Sarita Kendal, cofounder of Natütama. Sarita and her helpers worked over two years to restore the calf to health, feed it, care for it, and finally to wean it, so that it would be able to survive in the wild. The calf was named Airuwe, the Ticuna word for manatee.

The real Airuwe

Many people in Puerto Nariño got involved in Airuwe's care. He became a celebrity, and when it was time for him to be returned to the river, almost all the village came along. He was fitted with a radio collar so that Sarita and her team could track him and check that he was safe. At the same time, the collar gathered valuable information about manatee behavior. For several months, Sarita and a team of local fishermen spent hours every day watching Airuwe and learning about manatees.

Eventually Airuwe's collar dropped off, so it wasn't possible to keep track of him. But when a manatee was killed by the one local fisherman who had always been determined to keep hunting manatees, he was reported to the police and fled from the village.

Since that time, no one in Puerto Nariño nor its neighboring villages has killed a manatee. Fishermen and their families say that they will never hunt manatees, as they want their grandchildren to be able to see manatees as they themselves have always done.

Now all schoolchildren from Puerto Nariño, and

A Natütama educator
helps children learn about
their native wildlife.

from communities up and down the river and across
Colombia, visit Natütama's thatched headquarters. They
learn about manatees and the animals and plants that
share their environment by visiting an exhibition of

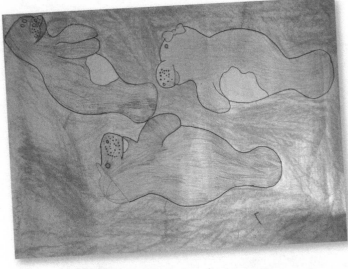

Child's picture of Airuwe

the manatees' underwater world and through songs, games, stories, and puppet shows. Natütama holds gala open-house days and takes part in local festivals. They even bake manatee cookies just like the ones in the book. Natütama workers visit villages across the border in Peru and Brazil to remind people of their connection with the natural world and the value of wildlife. Fishermen are employed to help monitor the small, precious population of about 35 manatees in the Puerto Nariño area, and they report over 500 sightings of manatees every year. Natútama's conservation work grows out of the community around it and encourages a culture of respectful stewardship, rather than exploitation.

Sarita was never sure if Airuwe had been killed. But to this day, people tell her that they've seen him upriver.

If you'd like to help keep manatees in the Amazon, you can support organizations like Natútama.

http://natutama.org/

E-mail: fundacionnatutama@yahoo.com